Contents

CHAPTER 1

Pappy Mashy always sat in the armchair.

It was the only comfortable chair. It was the only chair he could fit into. And he always read the newspaper.

The Mashy children – Josie,
Rosie, Gemma, Lisa, Tracy, Lacey,
Wayne, Elaine and little Arbuthnot
Mashy – played mostly.

And Mammy Mashy
did everything else.

She fed the cats,  shook the mats,

cooked the meals,  hushed the squeals,

kept bees,  pruned the trees,

taught the children their abc

fixed the roof,

unblocked the drains,

nursed the children's aches and pains,

ironed,

washed,

knitted,

sewed,

sang songs,

wrote letters,

changed nappies,

paid bills,

went to the supermarket,

mended punctures

and read the bedtime story.

13

And when the older children
were all safe in the classrooms of
Sloth Road School, the baby was
with Lilly-next-door and Pappy
Mashy had stumbled off to his office
to turn over more papers at his desk
all day, then she'd go out to her
part-time job as a bus driver.
But she always made sure she was
home in time to collect the children
and say hello to Pappy
as he sank into his
armchair to read
the evening papers.
Of course.

"Leave him be," she'd say to the little ones as she cooked the supper with one hand and did the big ones' homework with the other. "Your father's had a hard day."

That was just the way things were.

CHAPTER 2

Now, though he was fat, it wasn't
that Pappy Mashy was a lazy man.
It was just that he liked to read the
newspaper. And over the years, as
his family had grown larger and
larger, so he had come to like
reading the newspaper more and
more.

By the time little Arbuthnot was
born, Pappy Mashy didn't just read
one newspaper like most people.
He didn't just read two newspapers

like some people. He read lots of
newspapers. In fact he read every
newspaper he could lay his hands
on. There was:

There was:

And that was just to start with. You
name it, he read it, from the first
page to the last, every single word.

Pappy Mashy read so many
newspapers that the
paper-boy from the
shop down the road
had got a bad case
of soggy legs from
carrying them all
and refused to deliver
to number 23 any more.
So now, very early every morning,
the Mashy's front door would
open and out would come
Josie, Rosie, Gemma,
Lisa, Tracy, Lacey,
Wayne, Elaine
and little
Arbuthnot,

and they'd trot down the road to the
newspaper shop and stagger back
with a newspaper under each and
every arm.

And though Pappy Mashy was
too busy reading to play with them,
too busy reading to talk to them,
too busy reading even to notice
them, it wasn't that he didn't love
his children. It was only that he
couldn't resist the comfortable chair
and the pile of newspapers.

Chapter 3

The Mashy children were a clever lot and as busy as bees. They helped their mum. They helped their dad, and they certainly stood out at school.

Wayne and Elaine had nursery class helper badges for looking after the gerbils.

Tracy and Lacey loved dressing up.

Gemma
specialized
in weather
forecasting.

Josie could do
the crossword
faster than her
teacher, and knew
more long words;

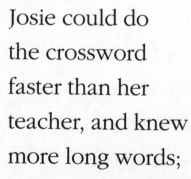

Lisa was into
art and
craft;

and Arbuthnot showed every sign
of taking after his father.

And Rosie? Rosie with
the red hair and the
bright blue eyes was
the cleverest of them
all. She noticed things.

CHAPTER 4

Now as the winter wore away and spring drew near Rosie did a lot of noticing.

She noticed that Mammy was getting thinner and thinner, while Pappy was getting fatter and fatter (so fat indeed that he could scarcely fit into the comfortable chair any more). And she noticed that Mammy was getting snappier and snappier, while Pappy was getting snoozier and snoozier.

So Rosie at least was not
surprised when one morning
Mammy Mashy just couldn't get up.

"I'm sorry," she said, lying there
in her bed, and her face was pale
pale pale, "I'b got a code id by dose
ad an ache id by head ad I feel
terrible."

Pappy Mashy was very worried. "I'm going to call the doctor," he said and thumped downstairs.

"Don't worry," said Josie. "We'll manage between us, won't we?"

"Yes," said Rosie, Gemma, Lisa, Tracy, Lacey, Wayne and Elaine in a chorus. Arbuthnot chuckled. "So stay in bed and have a good rest,"

said Rosie, leading them out.

A little while later Dr Porridge came to see Mammy Mashy. She spent a long time with her. On her way out she gave Pappy and the children their instructions: "She's to spend a week in bed," said Dr Porridge firmly, "a WHOLE week.

She's not to work, not to be worried, she's not even to come downstairs. What she needs is lots of warm drinks and peace and quiet and sleep. Is that clear?"

Josie, Rosie, Gemma, Lisa, Tracy, Lacey, Wayne, Elaine and little Arbuthnot all nodded solemnly. Even Pappy Mashy nodded, but his eyes were sliding towards the pages of the *Isfahan Gazette*.

CHAPTER 5

It was a desperate week.

Josie, Rosie, Gemma, Lisa, Tracy, Lacey, Wayne and Elaine worked like slaves, but no matter how hard they worked, still the dirty dishes piled up and the food supplies ran down and the drains got blocked and little Arbuthnot did unspeakable things when they weren't looking. And the tide of old newspapers rose and rose and swilled around the house threatening to engulf them all.

Pappy Mashy did try. He got up in the morning. He went to bed at night. He carried trays of warm drinks up to Mammy. He even fetched his own newspapers. But it took no more than a glimpse of his armchair for him to need a little read. And the little reads grew longer and longer until he was buried there almost as much as he had ever been.

"This will not DO!" said Rosie to Josie on Thursday night, as they swept a mountain of old paper out into the back yard.

"I'll give you a hand when I've finished this," mumbled Pappy

Mashy sheepishly from the depths of the comfortable chair.

Lacey was cross. "Humph!" she snorted. "He's just like the man in the story Mrs Bugwort told us at school, the man who was turned into stone."

"Except it's not stone he's been turned to," said Rosie, "it's newspaper!"

CHAPTER 6

By Friday they had eaten scrambled eggs six nights in a row, so Josie made pancake batter instead.

There was a gloomy silence in the kitchen, and they could hear the sound of Pappy sinking deeper into his papers next door.

"If only we could get him out of his chair," said Rosie.

"We had Miss Gullet for craft yesterday," piped up Lisa from the doorway.

"Really Lisa, is that all you can think about!" fretted Josie.

"Look out!" Elaine and Wayne staggered in with a pile of dirty washing. Wayne heaved it into the washing machine. Elaine lifted the

box of soap out on to the worktop.

"And we did papiyaay machaay," went on Lisa, unconcerned, "and Miss Gullet says there's going to be a craft competition and that I should make something for it."

Just then, Arbuthnot emptied a bag of flour on to the floor with spectacular results. He chortled. The kitchen filled with a cloud of dust and Josie, Rosie and Elaine all threw themselves on the floor to clear up the mess.

Seeing that they were busy,
Arbuthnot decided to improve the
batter mix. He leant over to the box
of soap powder, picked up a
scoopful and emptied it into the
mixing bowl.

The batter started
to froth.

"Oh no!" raged Josie,
straightening up, her hair white
with flour. "There goes supper and
we haven't got any eggs left!"

It was Rosie to the rescue. "No use crying over spilt milk," she said, removing the revolting Arbuthnot to the living room. Then she came back, picked up the mixing bowl and emptied it into the rubbish bin.

Lisa stared into the bin. Then she did something very odd. Instead of putting the lid back on, she reached her hand into the sticky mess of batter and newspaper and stirred.

"YUK!" shrieked Josie. "That's disgusting! What are you doing?" Elaine made sick noises.

Lisa lifted her hand out and let blobs of batter and paper drip.

"It's a bit like Miss Gullet's

papiyaay mashaay," she sang to herself with a little smile.

Rosie was noticing.

"Now I come to think of it," she said, "I seem to remember we did papier mâché when we were in Miss Gullet's too…"

Josie looked at them both as if they were mad.

"…and you can make models and things with it, can't you?"

"I'm hungry," wailed Wayne.

"All it is, is newspaper and flour-and-water paste, like batter without the eggs," said Lisa.

"And it goes all hard… As hard as stone," said Rosie thoughtfully.

"That's it!" she said, picking up a
handful of gloop out of the bin.
"Bother housework. I know what
we're going to do!"

And Rosie danced a war dance
on the sticky kitchen floor.

CHAPTER 7

So it was cold baked beans for supper, and Pappy didn't even notice. He was too busy reading the *Bogota Bulletin*.

"We'll clear up, Pappy," said Josie when they'd finished. "You take this hot drink up to Mum and keep her company for the evening." And Pappy, his nose still in his paper, obeyed like a lamb.

Then the fun began.

Such a ripping and tearing, a giggling and a scrunching you never did hear. Every waste-paper basket was emptied, every paper pile was plundered and soon the whole ground floor of no. 23 was filled with shreds and strips of torn newspaper.

Out in the kitchen Josie and
Gemma beat buckets
full of batter.

Arbuthnot played snowstorms in
the hall

and Rosie and Lisa were hard at
work dismantling the old rabbit run
and twisting the chicken wire that
covered it into a strangely familiar
shape.

All night long they worked,
pasting and patting, slopping and
sticking, while Arbuthnot slept in a
nest of cushions.

And when the first blackbird sang from the next door TV aerial, there was not a single newspaper, not even the tiniest shred of newspaper to be seen anywhere.

Josie, Rosie, Gemma, Lisa, Tracy, Lacey, Wayne and Elaine picked up little Arbuthnot and tiptoed upstairs to bed as the first cars revved in the street outside.

CHAPTER 8

When Pappy Mashy staggered downstairs that morning he thought he'd seen a ghost.

It wasn't just that the house was tidy. Nor even that there wasn't a single heap of newspapers to be seen.

It was THAT!

There in his armchair, the only comfortable armchair, in fact the only chair he could fit into nowadays, there was something …

someone ... sitting ... and
reading ... HIS newspaper!

Little Arbuthnot bumped down the stairs and landed at his feet.

"Pappy," said Arbuthnot stretching out his arms, and in his amazement Pappy Mashy actually bent down and picked him up! Arbuthnot gurgled happily and clapped his hands and Pappy became aware of a whole circle of sleepy children standing round him.

For the first time in a long time, Pappy Mashy looked straight at his children. They looked back expectantly.

Then, feeling weak at the knees
with so much effort, he turned
towards his chair again, and
groaned.

"Who IS that?"

"It's PAPIER MÂCHÉ!" said the
children in a chorus.

"Pappy Mashy?" whimpered Pappy, "but that's me!"

The children giggled.

Pappy Mashy went over to the figure in the chair.

"May I have my newspaper?" he asked.

The figure didn't move.

Pappy took hold of the newspaper.

It wouldn't move either.

So Pappy pulled. The newspaper ripped.

"Well at least let me have my chair!"

Pappy took the figure firmly by the arms. He tugged, he shook,

52

but all that happened was that the
chair lifted off the ground. The
figure was stuck fast.

And when he dropped it in despair, the whole lot landed on his foot.

Pappy hopped round the room in agony. The children were amazed. They couldn't ever remember him taking so much exercise in one morning.

But Tracy took no notice.

"Hey, Pappy," she said. "Come and look at this thing I've made, it's a superstrawbercoopercopter."

Pappy stopped hopping. "Huh?" he said.

And then he did another very unusual thing. Without a newspaper to read or a chair to sit in, Pappy DID look.

In fact, he did more than look. He
bent down and touched. Before
long he was vrooming the
superstrawbercoopercopter all over
the newspaper-free floor. Wonder
of wonders, Pappy was playing!

Pappy Mashy was so busy
playing that he didn't hear the
doorbell. He scarcely noticed Miss
Gullet come in, and when he saw
Josie and Rosie and Lisa help her
carry HIS chair out to the car for the

craft exhibition, he was having such a good time playing, that he just shrugged and waved.

"Phew!" he said as he mopped his face. "I haven't enjoyed myself so much for ages! Why don't you ask me to play with you more often?"

And Josie, Rosie, Gemma, Lisa, Tracy, Lacey, Wayne, Elaine and little Arbuthnot all laughed.

CHAPTER 9

That afternoon Mammy Mashy
came downstairs for the first time.
She was pale and weak but her face
seemed rested. The dark lines under
her eyes had gone and she looked
somehow rounder than before.

"Well, well," she said as she
looked around, "you have done a
good job!" Pappy smirked as if he'd
done it all himself. Josie kicked him.
"But where's the big chair gone?"

"Big chair?" asked Pappy, as if he'd never heard of it (and indeed he had almost forgotten it already), "It's er…"

"Being redecorated," said Lisa firmly. And that was the end of that.

But Rosie was noticing as usual.

"Are you sure you're all right, Mum?" she said. "You look a bit shaky."

"I do feel a bit weak," admitted Mammy. "I think, if you don't mind, I'll just have a little sit down."

And she sat down in the second most comfortable chair and opened a book.

MORE WALKER SPRINTERS
For You to Enjoy